CARLOS GOMEZ

FREESTYLES...
HEAVY ON THE STYLE

WRITTEN BY
CHUCK GONZALES

D0003449

TABLE OF CONTENTS

This book is for my mother, Mela Gonzales.

Preface

Hi! I'm Chuck Gonzales, the artist and writer. *Carlos Gomez Freestyles* is loosely based on my childhood in Sioux Falls, South Dakota. It is a lovely town which, at the time, was mostly filled with Anglos— white people. Which, given my Mexican-American heritage, I am not. This graphic novel exists in a time that is both current and also reflective of my childhood.

Because of when and where we were, I grew up without much LatinX cultural influence other than my immediate family, and was subjected to racism because of my dark skin and stiff black hair. In addition to my dark coloring, I had a pronounced lisp, no athletic ability, and, most importantly, a different sense of gender roles and sexuality than most of the kids around me. Which isn't always fun when you're just hoping to fit in. I also wanted to be as fabulously colorful as the pop stars I followed. None of whom looked anything like me. Basically, I wanted to be special AND not get picked on.

But it got better. I came to accept who and what I am despite, or because of, others' opinions. After a lot of work with a speech therapist, my lisp worked itself out. We left South Dakota for South Texas, where I went to high school and made great lifelong friends. I went on to college, became a professional illustrator and writer, traveled some, lived in Chicago, and met my husband, Michael. Who is the love of my life. We moved to New York City and have made a good life for ourselves. But I'm still pretty klutzy.

Carlos is a much braver and more colorful bird than I ever was. This book is the Hollywoodized version of my childhood I wished for. Since the story is semi-autobiographical, some characters are based on real people, some are a combination of people, some are complete fiction. This book is also a love letter to family members both alive and gone.

7

8

9

19

20

22

24

26

28

Chapter Three   Carlos

32

33

39

40

A mere 4 minutes later...

I SAVED THIS FOR MODESTY'S SAKE!

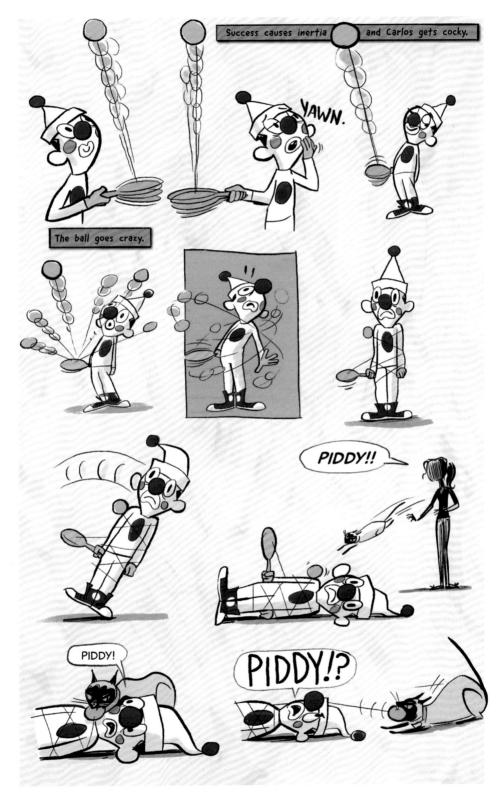

67

70

73

76

79

83

84

90

93

96

BMX

Carlos

102

105

113

114

115

116

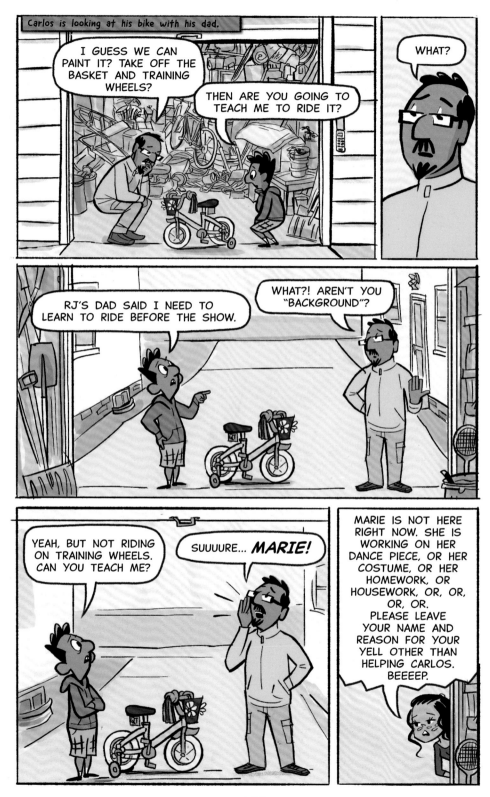

119

121

123

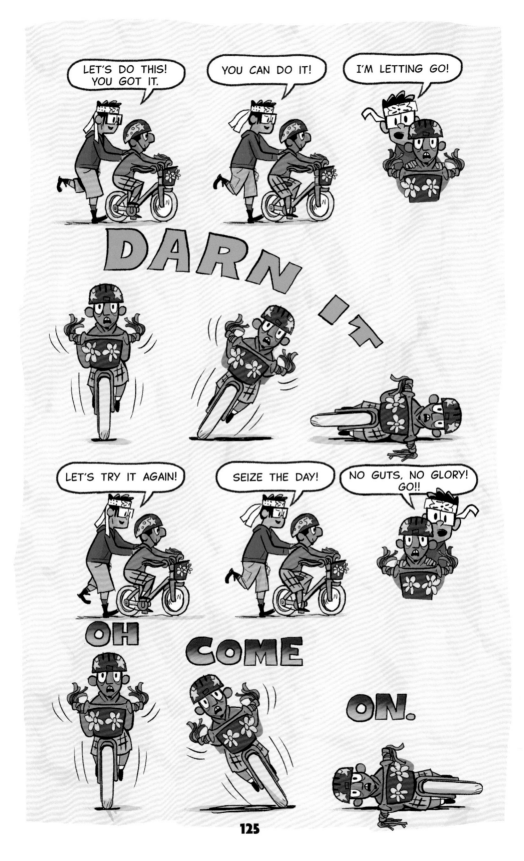

126

131

132

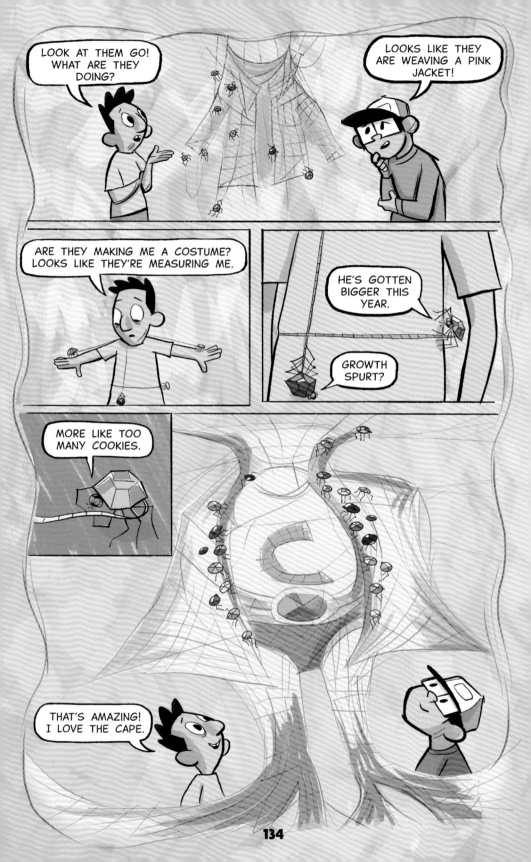

137

142

144

146

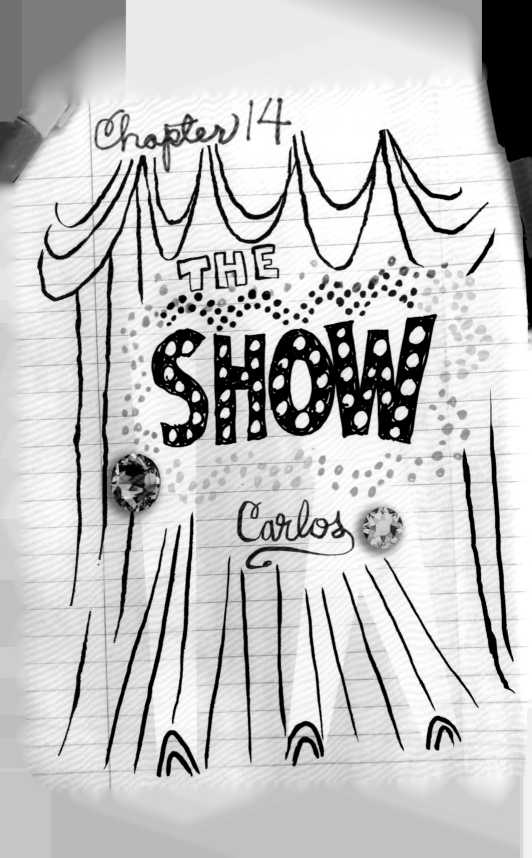

151

Panel 1 (left speech bubble): I GENERALLY COME IN THROUGH THE GYM, SO I WAS UNAWARE. THAT'S GREAT THAT HE'S CREATIVE, BUT HE HAS A TOUGH TIME FITTING IN.

Panel 1 (right speech bubble): BEING STOOD IN FRONT OF CLASS WHILE OTHER STUDENTS ARE TOLD NOT TO MAKE FUN OF YOU DOESN'T EXACTLY HELP ONE FIT IN.

Caption: The lights go down and it's show time!

Speech bubble: CAN I PLEASE GET EVERYONE'S ATTENTION? THANK YEW THANK YEW THANK YEW, PREFERRED PRONOUNS! WELCOME TO THE ENTERTAINMENT PORTION OF THIS YEAR'S RV SHOW! THE CIVIC MINDED FOLKS AT THE KEYTOMA CLUB COLLECTED QUITE A WACKY LINE UP FOR THIS YEAR'S TALENT COMPETITION!

WE'VE GOT DARLENE AND HER AUTOHARP! STUMPY AND HIS CLASSICAL CHAINSAW SCULPTING. WE'VE GOT FLY FISH'N, DANCING BY MARIE AND JUAN, AND A GREAT BMX BIKING EXPO-SI-TION!

WITH NO FURTHER ADO...

155

156

158

159

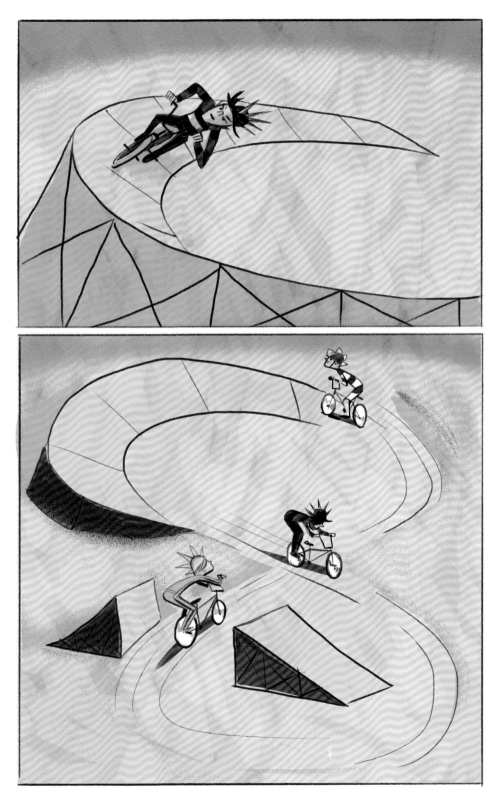

166

THE CELEBRATION

chapter 15

WAGON WHEEL

Carlos

Gross Jello

Oozy Fish

Putrid Peas

Nasty Noodles

178

186